GREEN DREAMS

by

J.M.R. Meagher

Watermill Press

Printed in the United States of America

Illustrations by James R. Odbert

ISBN 0-89375-825-6

CONTENTS

Finn's Dragon

Long ago, many places had dragon trouble now and then. Dragons would come and frighten everyone. Then they would move on. But the dragon of Antrim came to stay. He was not like most dragons. He didn't make a pile of treasure and go to sleep. He stayed awake. And he stayed hungry. He was ruining the kingdom.

The king of Antrim made an offer. Half his kingdom would go to whomever could rid Antrim of the dragon. The king also promised the Princess Ann in marriage. Ann was the king's only child. She was tall, and her hair was golden. Many men had dreamed of marrying her.

When word went out of the king's offer, men started coming from all over to try their luck. Many of them were princes and lords. Some of them even came from over the seas. One by one, they rode off to challenge the dragon. Not one ever came back. Gloom deepened.

There was a poor shepherd called Finn. He lived in the north of Antrim, far from where the dragon was. Finn had no sheep of his own. He made a living for himself and his widowed mother

6

by tending other people's sheep.

Though poor, he was known as Finn the Lucky. He always seemed to know where to look for a lost sheep or a stray goat. Once, too, he caught a fat trout and found a copper coin in its belly.

"Lucky!" Finn laughed. "If I were lucky, I would have found a gold coin. If I were lucky, I would have a few sheep to call my own."

"Never mind, Finn," said pretty Mary, the miller's daughter. She and Finn had grown up together. "At least you're not a prince or a lord. If you were, you'd feel you had to go off and fight the dragon."

Right away, she knew she'd said the wrong thing. A strange light came into Finn's eyes. "I could do it," he said. "I could be the one to get rid of that beast."

"Now, Finn," said Mary, with a shake of her dark hair. "You don't even have a

*Right away, Mary knew she'd said
the wrong thing.*

sword of your own."

It was no use trying to talk him out of it. The next day, Finn set out on foot for the king's house. His mother packed him some food. She kissed her son and told him to be careful.

Mary was there to see him off. "Won't you wish me luck?" Finn said.

"Finn," said Mary, "you have enough luck already. And if your luck holds, or your luck fails, it's all the same."

"Not for me," Finn said. He was thinking of the dragon.

"I'll never see you again, either way," Mary said. She was thinking of the Princess Ann.

So Finn came to the king's house. He could see no one thought much of his chances against the dragon. But he met with the tall princess. It was easy to understand why so many men would risk their lives for her. The latest had been a prince, who came all the way from Norway. He had ridden off a week ago to find the dragon. No one had seen him since.

Most dragons live in wild and lonely places. But the dragon of Antrim had more sense. He'd found himself a cave where the main road ran through some woods. That way, his food came to him.

So Finn found the dragon without much trouble. At first, he wasn't sure it *was* the dragon. It didn't look much like the pictures of dragons Finn had seen in books. His wings were much larger. And he didn't have those stumpy little legs. This dragon's legs were long, like a goat or a horse. But they did have claws.

The dragon was lying half-inside his cave. As Finn came near, he opened his great wide mouth. A low growl and a

The dragon was lying half-inside his cave.

wisp of smoke came out together. Then Finn was fairly sure he had the right address. The teeth of the beast were like knives.

"How are you today, sir?" Finn asked.

"I'm well enough," the dragon growled. "And yourself?"

Finn shook his head sadly. "I'm well enough," he said. "But I'm a disappointed man. I've heard many terrible things about dragons. But never that they had bad manners."

The dragon looked offended. He showed his teeth. "How can you say that? Didn't I just ask about your health?" he said. "I could have eaten you without a word."

Finn gathered up his courage. "You aren't wanted here," he said. "Is it good manners to stay where you are not wanted?"

"I'm not wanted anywhere, if it comes to that," the dragon said. He grinned.

"That's where you're wrong," said Finn. "You're wanted in Meath."

"Meath?"

"All the young men in Meath," Finn went on, "think they are great dragon-fighters. Perhaps you have noticed that they are all coming to Antrim. They haven't had a dragon of their own for years." Finn wasn't exactly telling the truth.

"And where is Meath?" asked the dragon.

"South," Finn replied. It was about all he really knew about Meath. "It's south of here."

Finn was in luck again. Winter was coming on. The dragon was starting to feel the chill. Fire in a dragon's belly does not keep out the cold. Now, this

13

dragon had once spent a happy century in Spain. He still remembered the warm southern sun. As it happened, Meath was not so far south of Antrim. The winters were just like the ones in Antrim. But the word *south* had stirred the dragon's memories. He came a little farther out of his cave. He spread his great wings and flapped once.

"South," he was muttering, "south. And the lads think themselves dragon-fighters."

About a week later, there was a great commotion in Finn's village. Finn was back! He was riding a horse and driving a small flock of sheep. He said they were his own.

He went straight to the mill. Mary was there.

"Did you get rid of the dragon?" she asked.

Finn was riding a horse and driving a small flock of sheep.

"I did," he said, and he told his tale. "So the dragon," he finished, "flapped about in a great circle. Then he headed south. Whether he's in Meath or Morocco now is anyone's guess. The main point is, he's gone from Antrim."

Mary was proud of Finn the Lucky. She asked, "Are you lord of half the kingdom now? Should I bow to you and call you '*sir*'?" She didn't look as if she would do either.

Finn shook his head. "I said to the king, 'What would I do with half the kingdom? I was never trained to be a king. I'd make a mess of it. I wouldn't sleep nights as I do now. A little flock of sheep would be more use to me, Your Majesty.' So that's what he gave me — that, a horse, and this suit of clothes." It was the first new suit of clothes Finn had ever owned.

16

"You look fine," Mary allowed. "But what about the Princess Ann? How can you marry her and stay a shepherd?"

"Well," Finn said, "I had a private word with the princess."

"Is she as lovely as they say?" Mary asked.

"Lovelier," Finn said. "And she liked me, well enough. But I could see her heart was set on someone else. So I told her I could never marry her."

"Was she angry?" Mary asked.

"She was very pleased," Finn replied. "She gave me gifts. She gave me a bag of gold. And she gave me this." From his pack, he pulled out a fine linen gown. It was a gown a princess might wear, or a lucky woman on her wedding day.

"The Princess Ann," Finn went on, "said I might get married someday. Perhaps she could tell."

"Tell what?"

He looked into Mary's dark eyes. "That my heart was set on someone else, too," Finn said.

Mary measured the gown against herself. "I would just have to take up the hem a little," she said, smiling.

That's where the tale of Finn's dragon ends.

Watch Out
for the Water

Not long ago, most homes had no running water. Water was drawn each day from the well. When hot water was needed, it was heated on the stove. After the water had been used, it was thrown out the door. Of course, you had to look where you threw it.

At night, it was the custom to shout, "Watch out for the water!" Throwing water out at night could be very risky. It might fall on an evil spirit. And then the spirit's revenge would be swift. The night is full of spirits. They do not like to get wet.

One dark night, a woman was cooking her evening meal. Her name was Molly O'Dea. Molly was weary, and for good reason. She was the mother of six children. She was often too busy to notice what she was doing. Sometimes she would put on socks that didn't match. Sometimes she would put sugar in her soup and salt in her coffee. She was always losing things. And on this night, she was busier and more mixed up than usual.

One of Molly's children was in bed with a cold. Everything was going wrong. Before supper, she had been dyeing wool in a pot. Now she needed the pot for something else. She took the pot from the stove. She carried it to the door. And with barely a glance, she threw it out. In her hurry, she forgot to shout, "Watch out for the water!"

As soon as she let go of the water, there was a terrible scream. Molly looked everywhere. But there was no one in sight. At once she knew what she had done. She had thrown the hot water on an evil spirit.

When her husband Tom came home, Molly told him everything. Tom turned white with fear. But all they could do was wait for the angry spirit to return. They got very little sleep that night.

Morning came and they were safe. "Perhaps it was nothing after all," they said to each other. But the fear stayed

Molly forgot to shout, "Watch out for the water!"

with them.

Tom came home early that night. It had been a good day and he was in good spirits. So was Molly. But as it grew dark, there was fear in their eyes. They hardly spoke during supper. Even their six children were quiet.

When the children were finally in bed, Tom and Molly sat by the fire. They were silent and stared into the flames. Then, they heard a sound at the door. *It's probably the wind,* they thought. But the sound came again. Molly looked at Tom. Tom nodded and went to the door. It would be worse to keep a spirit waiting.

When Tom opened the door, a black lamb ran in past him. Its back had been badly burned. Molly and Tom watched the lamb in terror. Surely it was the evil spirit of the night before. But it seemed

Tom and Molly sat by the fire.

to mean no harm. It walked to the fire and lay down. It moaned with pain. And then it died.

Now, Molly and Tom were kind people. It hurt them to see the poor animal suffer. Tom picked up the lamb in his arms. He carried it behind the house. There, he made a grave for it.

Could this be the end of the spirit? he wondered. He and Molly were not so sure it was.

The next night, Tom came home early again. Once more, the family was quiet at supper. They wondered what the night would bring.

After supper, Molly and Tom sat by the fire without a word. An hour passed, then two hours. Then the sound came again at the door. This time, they both went. When they opened the door, the same black lamb ran in. As it had the night before, it lay by the fire in pain. Once more, it died.

Tom carried the lamb back to its grave. When he dug it open, he found it empty. So he lay the lamb inside again and covered it quickly. Now they knew how the spirit would punish them. It would attack the tenderest part of their hearts. They must do something. They could not bear to see the poor beast again without helping it.

Luckily, there was a wise man in the village. He had dealt with spirits before. Tom and Molly went to him with their tale. The wise man went to his books. After a great deal of study, he found a way to solve the problem. Without saying a word, he mixed together many powders and potions.

"Take this salve," he said at last. "Say this to the lamb: 'Lamb, I am sorry for

Without saying a word, the wise man
mixed together many powders and potions.

your hurt. But I will not bury you again. Instead, I will cure you.' Then put this salve on its back. But you must act quickly. If you don't, it will come again and again."

That night, Tom and Molly got ready. When the sound came, Molly opened the door. Tom seized the lamb.

"Lamb," Tom said, "I am sorry for your hurt. But I will not bury you again. Instead, I will cure you." And he put the salve on the lamb's back.

The burn healed at once. And the lamb ran out into the night.

From then on, the whole town could hear Molly O'Dea. "Watch out for the water!" she would shout. No matter how busy she became, she never forgot again.

The Five Brothers

In a kingdom far away, there was once a dark time when the land was without a king. Without a leader, all was confusion. The land turned barren. Fields that were once green turned to sand. And from this sand, the people had to scrape a bare living.

The trouble was with the old king's sons. The king died before any of his sons had married. There were five of them. And it was the law of the land that none could become king until he had a wife. None of the five wanted to get married. They enjoyed the wild life. They liked to hunt and fish and roam about the country. Besides, they said, they could find no women good enough to suit them.

"A king's wife should be as bright as the sun," said James.

"She must be tender as a flower petal," John chimed in.

"Her hair should be like silk," William added.

"She should have the soul of an angel," Michael suggested.

"And she must be fair and faithful,"

*The five sons liked to hunt and fish and
roam about the country.*

Brian concluded.

To this, they all cheered. They were quite sure they would never find such a woman. And that is exactly what they hoped.

Meanwhile, things grew worse in the land. Many people died of hunger.

Then it happened that, after a day of hunting, the brothers found themselves thirsty and without water. So James went to search for some. After wandering about, he managed to find a well. Beside it sat an ugly old woman. James decided to ignore the woman. Without saying a word to her, he took hold of the well bucket. But as hard as he tried, he couldn't move it.

"This is my well," said the old woman. "You cannot draw water without my permission."

"Then I ask your permission," James

said. He was rather rude about it.

"You may have water for a kiss and a promise of marriage," replied the old woman.

The thought of marriage to her terrified James. So he ran off in search of another well. But he couldn't find one.

"There is no water," James told his brothers, "except for a well guarded by an old woman. And for her water, she wants a promise of marriage."

"We will see about this," John laughed. "Come, Michael," he said to his brother. "Let us talk to the old woman." And the two men went on their way.

They soon found the old woman and the well. First, they tried the bucket. It wouldn't move. Then they tried to persuade the woman. But she insisted on her kiss and promise of marriage. Of course, the brothers would have none of

They tried to persuade the woman.

this and they left.

By this time, they were all quite thirsty. So William and Brian decided to try the old woman. They pleaded and argued. They used sweet talk and threats. But the old woman stood firm. No marriage, no water.

"It is not for me," she said at last. "It is for the kingdom. Without a wife, none of you can be king. And without a king, the land will remain barren."

The brothers thought about this. She was right, of course. But marriage to such a woman would be impossible. Their thirst grew worse.

Then, William, who was quite brave, seized the old woman and kissed her lightly on the cheek.

"There," he said. "Now will you give us water?"

"It's a fair start," the old woman said,

"but it's not good enough. I want my promise of marriage."

William could do no more, and he turned away. Brian knew it was up to him. He thought of his thirst. Then he thought for the first time of the people of the kingdom. They suffered, too. And their suffering was far worse than his own.

"I will marry you," Brian cried at last. Then he kissed the old woman full on the mouth.

Immediately, the bucket came loose from its place. And the old woman changed into a young woman of shining beauty. She was a goddess!

She and Brian were married, and the land bloomed again. What had been sand turned to rich earth. There was food and drink enough for all once again.

*The old woman changed into a young woman
of shining beauty.*

Brian and his wife reigned as king and queen for fifty years. Their children and grandchildren reigned for 500 years after that. And all this time, the land remained green and beautiful.

The Man with a Hump

There was once a poor basket weaver named Ben. He was a plain and simple man. He worked hard for his living. He made lovely baskets, and they were much in demand. But Ben himself was not much in demand. He lived alone in a tiny cottage. He had been born with a crooked back. He walked hunched over.

And on his back, there was a large hump. He had a kind face and bright blue eyes. But no one seemed to notice his smile or his eyes. All anyone could see was the hump. People just thought of him as a poor unfortunate fellow.

Ben worked hard all day. But in the evening, he was lonely. So he often took walks through the valley and along the river. One summer night, he was taking such a walk. He was about to turn back for his cottage. Then he heard a strange sound in the distance. He stood very still and strained to hear. It was singing. The moon was full. The valley was covered in a soft, pale light. He followed the sound across the valley. He made sure to walk very softly. He took care not to be seen. He didn't want to frighten the singers. Finally, he drew very near to the singers. What he saw made him gasp with surprise.

Ben saw before him in the valley a group of elves. They were singing and dancing with great delight. They formed a circle and held hands. They danced round and round. And always they sang the same words to the same tune. "Monday and Tuesday, Monday and Tuesday," went the words. Ben found the song to be very boring. After a while, he couldn't bear it any longer. He couldn't help himself. He sang with them and added ". . . and Wednesday."

At once, the singing and dancing stopped. The elves were startled to be joined by anyone else. But they were delighted with what Ben added to their song. For one thing, Ben had a lovely voice. And for another thing, what he added made sense to them. Over and over, they sang "Monday and Tuesday

The valley was flooded in a soft, pale light.

and Wednesday." They liked it. They liked it very much.

Suddenly, a great wind rose in the valley. It had been called up by the elves. The wind closed in on Ben and spun him round and round. He could see and hear nothing. The wind lifted him off his feet. He was carried off. Moments later, the wind dropped him to the ground. He was very dizzy. At first, he could see nothing but swirls, and he could not get his balance. Then he saw a ring of elves all around him. As he stood up, he noticed something wonderful. He was standing perfectly tall and straight. His hump was gone! The elves had rewarded him for what he had given them. Ben was grateful to them. Ben and the elves smiled at each other. And they sang and danced through the night. "Monday and Tuesday and Wednesday."

The next morning, Ben returned to town. In fact, he ran through the town. And the townspeople could not believe their eyes. He ran tall and straight. His hump had slid away. People began to notice his sparkling blue eyes. And his smile charmed them. Suddenly, Ben seemed to be the most popular person in town. People were sorry they had not gotten to know Ben sooner. Of course, he told his tale far and wide. Some people believed him. Some did not. But no one doubted that his hump was gone. That much was plain to see.

The strange story of Ben spread to all the nearby towns. One day, there was a knock on Ben's door. It was an old woman. She had come a long way. Ben sat her down and gave her some tea.

"I have come to help a friend," she said. "My friend has a son with a large

Ben ran tall and straight.

nose. Perhaps the elves will make it smaller for him. Tell me the whole story of how the elves helped you."

Ben was glad to tell his story to the old woman. She listened to every word. Then she thanked him, stood up, and left.

Several days later, the son of the friend of the old lady came to Ben. "Show me where the elves dance and sing," he commanded. His name was Jack, and his manner was gruff.

Ben pointed to the valley at the foot of the mountain. "Over there," he said.

Without a word of thanks, Jack set out. He walked a few miles before he heard the song of the elves in the distance. He drew nearer. They were dancing and singing merrily, "Monday and Tuesday and Wednesday."

"And Thursday!" shouted Jack. He had the voice of a bull. It was all noise

A great wind roared around Jack.

and no tone. He was bad tempered and impatient to be done with the business.

The elves screamed with surprise and anger. They were enraged at this rude interruption. Again a great wind rose in the valley. It roared around Jack. It drew him up into the sky and spun him like a top. Then it dropped him to the ground with a thud.

When Jack came to, he felt his face. His nose was certainly smaller. He felt again. Then he screamed in terror. What he found was that he had no nose at all.

"I must have done something wrong," said Jack. "I must have done something wrong!" But he never guessed what it was.

Ben could have told him. But he figured it would be no use. Jack would have to learn the reason for himself.

The Magic Zither

"I'll go see Martha," Lily said. "That's what I'll do."

Folks didn't go to see Martha often. They only went when they had a problem. For one thing, Martha lived on top of a mountain. It was a long way, and it was all uphill.

For another thing, Martha was different. In fact, she was a bit scary to some folks. They said she was a witch. But she wasn't. She was simply a wise person who could foretell the future.

Martha was a good listener. Listening carefully, she could understand people's problems. It was this that made her wise. But telling the future was another matter. For this, she used her zither.

A zither is a musical instrument. It looks a bit like a flat guitar without a handle. It has thirty or forty strings. To play it, you hold it in your lap. Then you pluck the strings. It is a very old instrument. And Martha's zither was said to be a magic one.

"I've seen her flying across the moon on it," one old man said. "She looked like a witch on a broom."

But the old man must have been dreaming. Martha never flew anywhere. All she used the zither for was to make music. And she would tell futures when someone asked.

Lily Jones had a problem for Martha. She wanted to get married. And just anyone wouldn't do. She wanted to marry Robert Moore.

Robert was handsome. Robert's father was rich. And more than once, it seemed to Lily, Robert had let her know he liked her. But would he marry her? That was the question. She felt she had to know. And since she couldn't tell the future herself, she thought of Martha.

Because it was a long way, she had to set out early. So she was surprised to meet her friend Carey Rudd.

"Carey!" Lily said. "What are you doing out so early?"

"I'm off to see Martha," Carey said. "How about you?"

The girls were pleased to find they were going the same way. It would be good company for the long trip. Each knew the other had a problem. That would be the only reason to see Martha. But neither would ask the other what the problem was. It wouldn't have been polite to pry, after all. They might have been surprised to find they both had the same problem.

They had just gone a bit farther when Della Newton came out of her house. "Wait!" she called. "I'll walk with you. I'm going the same way."

It turned out, of course, that she was on her way to Martha's house, too. And, of course, she had the same problem as the others. She had her heart set on Robert Moore.

"I'm off to see Martha," Carey said.

Before long, there were six girls on their way to see Martha. As chance would have it, they all wanted to marry Robert Moore. This would be quite a problem, even for a wise woman like Martha.

It was noon when they arrived. Martha was in her front yard to greet them. She had seen them trudging up the mountain.

"Good day to you, ladies," she said to them. "It's a pleasant day to have so much company."

The girls were shy, so Martha got right to the point. "You all have problems," she said. The girls nodded their heads yes. "Well, we'll see what we can do about them. They are problems of the heart, if I'm not mistaken."

The girls were amazed at Martha's wisdom. *How could she have known?*

they wondered.

"Perhaps you know," Martha went on, "that all of you have the same problem." The girls didn't know. They looked at one another with their mouths hanging open. Martha added, "You all want to marry Robert Moore."

Martha sat back to enjoy the effect her words had on the girls. After the first shock, they chattered among themselves. Each argued it couldn't be true. Robert had made certain promises. Then they agreed to leave it up to Martha. She was so wise. She had known all along.

The fact was, Martha was something of a humbug. She was good at guessing. She knew that Robert Moore was causing trouble for all the girls in town. And she was sure that in time her advice would be asked by some of them. But she was surprised to see all six at once. But when she did, she was all the more sure what the problem was.

"Well," she said at last. "I suppose it's time to predict the future. Who shall have him?" The girls grew silent.

"I can't take you all at once, though," Martha said. "Lily Jones, you first. The rest of you wait outside."

Lily trembled as she waited for what would happen next. It's not easy to face your future. Martha got her zither and began to play. It was an eerie and haunting tune. Then she sang:

"Zither, zither, tell me whether
Robert Moore will come to tether;
Can Lily make this man her own?
Come! The future must be known."

Martha stopped playing. She stood up and placed the zither on the sill of an open window. "There," she said. "The

Martha got her zither and began to play.

zither will soon give us an answer."

Lily gasped as the zither began to play by itself. It was the strangest music she had ever heard. It seemed to come from out of this world. Martha listened to the music and nodded her head. It was clear to Lily that the zither was saying something.

When she had heard enough, Martha took up the zither. It stopped playing at once. Then she smiled at Lily.

"You shall have him," she said. "Robert Moore is yours."

Lily was beside herself with joy. She couldn't believe her good fortune. But Martha had said it. So it must be true.

"Ah, poor child," Martha said. She patted Lily's arm as though she pitied her.

"Poor child? Why 'poor child'?" Lily asked. "I have everything my heart

58

desires. I couldn't be happier."

"Good, good," Martha said. "I'm glad you love him so deeply. The zither also says he will be poor and ill. Robert will soon lose his wealth. He will need your love."

At this news, Lily gave a little cry. She ran from the room. When the other girls saw her they thought, "Poor Lily." And they figured their own chances were so much better. Lily never stopped to tell them why she was upset. She ran sobbing all the way home.

One by one, Martha spoke to the girls. One by one, they ran crying down the mountain. Since not one of them waited for the others, not one knew they had all been told the same thing.

As it turned out, none of the girls married Robert Moore. The next time he went calling on Lily Jones, she refused

Lily ran sobbing all the way home.

to see him. One by one, he tried the other girls. It was the same everywhere. In the end, when he was ready to marry and settle down, he had to find a wife in another town. None of the local girls would have him.

Robert never did lose his fortune. And he was as happy and as healthy as most people in the world. Some of the girls married well and some didn't. Some were happy with their lives and some weren't. But what about Martha's wisdom? And what about the magic zither? Were they worthless after all?

It depends upon how you look at it. Martha, as it has been said, was a humbug. But she was a clever and wise humbug. She knew none of the girls loved Robert. It was his money they loved. Robert, she decided, needed to be taught a lesson. He was playing too many girls on his string.

Speaking of strings—the zither always played weird music when it was set in an open window. It was the wind blowing across the strings.

THE LOON

Nim was court jester to King Malcolm. Nim was kept to amuse the lords and the ladies.

In those days, a jester was also called a loon. Men who could be made fun of were picked for the job. They did not have to be funny as long as they looked or acted in a way that seemed foolish. A crippled man might be a good jester.

Someone simple or slow-witted might also be chosen. It was a cruel kind of fun these people enjoyed.

Nim was not slow-witted. In fact, he was very bright. He had been named Nim for his nimble mind. He was, however, crippled from birth. It was his back. And this made him limp and lean over as he walked.

Nim couldn't work on his father's farm. And no one would teach him a trade. On market days, people poked fun at him. It was a poor life at best for Nim.

Nim's father decided to take him to the royal court. If Nim could be a jester, it would be no worse. He would at least have food and a place to live. The family was too poor to keep him at home.

So it was done. The king's steward decided Nim would make a fine jester.

He dressed him in a patchwork costume. He put a funny hat on his head. He gave him bells and rattles to play with. And Nim was a jester—or loon.

"A loon must never look sad," he was told. "You are our jester. It won't do to make people sorry for you."

Nim did his best. He hopped and rolled about. He was jolly and foolish and amusing. In other words, he did quite well as a jester.

But one person at court was sorry for Nim. Behind the fun, she saw his sadness. This was Lady Margaret. Margaret, or Maggie, was the daughter of an earl.

She saw Nim one day in the garden. He didn't know she was watching him. Nim held a rose. And he was crying softly.

"Why are you so sad?" she asked. "You

And Nim was a jester—or loon.

are our jester, are you not?"

"I'm sorry that I'm not merry," Nim said. "But a man cannot always act like a loon, even though he is called one. Wait a bit and I'll hop about. I'll roll on the ground and shake my rattle for you."

"No. Please, Nim, don't. I'm sorry," Lady Margaret said. For the first time, she saw more than Nim's funny suit. His face was handsome. His eyes were intelligent. She thought she would like to talk to him some more.

"I thought it was the rose that made you sad," she said.

"It is, my lady," Nim replied. "Indeed it is the rose. Here is a thing not much more than a weed. Still, it is straight and lovely. I am a man. But I am twisted and ugly. It hardly seems fair."

"I have seen many roses with twisted stems," Maggie said. "Perhaps you are one of those. Your face is handsome. You are surely a clever fellow. Who knows? You may be a rose after all."

Maggie smiled at Nim. She touched his face gently. And then she kissed him.

Nim was greatly moved by Maggie's kindness. He gave her the rose and hobbled off. A jester must not fall in love with a lady.

Maggie watched him go. She looked at the rose and began to cry herself. *This must be a weeping rose,* she thought. And she held it to her face. "Poor loon," she whispered. "I'm afraid I'm in love with you."

Maggie would find Nim often in the garden. They knew they loved one another. But if the rest of the court knew...! It would be the funniest joke of all. The loon was in love with Lady

This must be a weeping rose, *Maggie thought.*

Margaret! It was impossible. But it had happened. And for Nim, it was the only thing that made life worth living.

Then, quite suddenly, Maggie stopped coming to the garden. There was an air of mystery about the court. Something was about to happen.

The steward told Nim there would be a banquet. "It is a matter of great importance," he said. "We will have a foreign guest. A treaty has been made. Be sure you are at your best. It is a fine and happy occasion for us all."

The guest was King Henry. He was the ruler of a large kingdom to the north. Henry was known as a cruel man. But he was powerful. He would be a good ally for King Malcolm and his people.

The banquet was a great success. Nim did what was expected. He was great fun for the merry crowd. The guest of honor was a tall and handsome man. Only his eyes were hard. Maggie sat next to him. She looked pale and afraid. She wouldn't eat, and she wouldn't drink with the rest. Nim sensed that something terrible was about to happen.

King Malcolm rose and called for silence. "We have great news," he said. "There is at last a treaty between our two kingdoms. And to seal the pact, one of our own will become King Henry's queen. Let's have a toast to Lady Margaret, the future queen."

Everyone rose and cheered. But above the cheering, there was a strange and eerie sound. At first, it sounded like a howl. Then it turned to wild laughter. And finally, it was a mixture of both. The crowd froze and turned toward the

*"Let's have a toast to Lady Margaret,
the future queen."*

source of the noise.

It was Nim. He seemed to be putting on the best act of his life. He rolled on the floor and his bells jingled. But the sounds he made were not funny. It was all pain and grief.

"Has the loon gone mad?" someone asked.

"I think the good news has overheated his brain," said another.

"Let's cool him off," a young noble suggested. "Into the lake with him."

They all thought that would be good fun. So Nim was dragged off to the lake. In the noise and excitement, no one heard Maggie screaming.

Nim was cast into the water. Down he went into the depths of the lake. The jokers laughed and waited for him to swim to the surface. But he never came up.

Instead, a large ducklike bird appeared. It had a handsome black head and bright eyes. On its back were patches of black and white like a jester's cloak. When it gave its call, it was all too familiar to the young nobles. They fell silent to listen. It began as a wail. Then there was wild laughter. And then it wailed again. It was Nim, they said, changed into a bird.

So they called it a loon. And when the bird rose to fly, they noticed it flew as if it had a humped back. It was the bird we still call a loon today. If you are in the northern woods, you can hear it. It still laughs and wails as Nim did the night he lost Lady Margaret.

The Man Who Didn't Like Fish

As everyone knows, Ireland is surrounded by the sea. It is an island. As you might expect, people there eat a lot of fish. It is sad to live in Ireland and not like fish, especially if you live by the sea.

Bobby Kildare was just such a man.

He lived in a fishing village. And he didn't like fish. Or, at least that's what he thought. He had never tasted fish in his life.

Bobby's neighbors all loved fish. Many of them were fishermen. So they tried to coax Bobby at least to try some.

"Leave me be!" he would shout at them. "I don't like large fish or small fish. I'll eat neither clams nor oysters. I will not look at a crab or a lobster. The sight of fish disgusts me. They look as if they come from the devil himself. And they smell worse!"

"Watch what you say, Bobby Kildare," he was told many times. "You'll bring a curse upon all of us. You should be grateful for the bounty of the sea."

But Bobby would not watch what he said. As long as there were fish, he would speak against them.

This was a very dangerous thing to do. In Ireland, there are more ears to hear than you can see. There are spirits and creatures who listen to catch a man in foolish talk. They were listening to Bobby.

One night, Bobby went out for a walk. He was passing a field of wild roses when he thought he heard a noise. He stopped to listen. At first, it sounded like a breeze in the grass. But it wasn't. Listening closely, he knew it was music. Then looking closely, he saw a group of Little People. They were playing instruments, and they were singing.

Bobby was frightened. A chill shivered down his spine. But he was also curious. Not many folks had ever seen the Little People. He tried to hear the words of their song:

"Oh for a life on the rolling sea. . ."

*The Little People were playing instruments,
and they were singing.*

As he listened, the music seemed to grow louder. The Little People seemed to grow bigger. But they were not getting bigger. Bobby was getting smaller!

When Bobby was as small as the Little People, the music stopped. The Little People cheered and welcomed him. "Hurrah!" they cried. "A guest! We have a guest!"

Just then, a large table appeared. There were fifty chairs around the table. At once, the Little People set about preparing for a huge feast. They laid out fine linen on the table. On this, they set their best china and glasses. Next to these, they laid out gleaming silver knives and forks.

Bobby was asked to sit at the head of the table. He was the guest of honor. A trumpet was blown and the first course arrived. It was brought in a silver bowl by two chefs. A footman waited to serve. It was soup — fish chowder, to be exact.

As guest of honor, Bobby was expected to take the first sip of soup. Only then could the others begin. But Bobby refused to try it.

"I do not like fish," he announced. "And I do not like fish chowder."

A silence fell about the table. The Little People were shocked. How could a guest of honor act so? With an angry shout, the Little People threw their bowls of chowder at Bobby.

Bobby tried to get up and run for his life. But he couldn't. He found he was stuck to his chair. And the chair was stuck to the ground.

After a while, the Little People calmed down. The signal was given for the second course. "This is a rare treat," they told Bobby. "You are sure to like it."

"I do not like fish," Bobby announced.

It was brought out on a large silver tray. Generous portions were served to all. It was a crab-meat salad.

Again, Bobby refused to eat. And again, the Little People stared in shocked silence. In a rage, they flung their salads at Bobby. The crab meat turned into live crabs. And the crabs crawled all over Bobby. They pinched his ears, and they clung to his nose and pulled on his hair. Bobby screamed and shouted until finally they were gone. He decided he would surely eat whatever came next.

The trumpet sounded. Four chefs and eight footmen arrived. They carried a huge silver tray. This was the main course. Carefully, they set it before Bobby. As guest of honor, he was to take the first piece.

A footman lifted the cover of the tray. It was a huge baked swordfish. Bobby thought he knew what would happen if he refused this. He would almost certainly be run through by the fish's sword. So he helped himself to the tiniest bit of swordfish.

Bobby's hosts looked at him in silence. They did not approve. Frightened at what might happen, Bobby took a larger helping. It still seemed not enough. So he filled his plate. The Little People smiled and clapped their hands. This was more like it.

When all were served, they waited for Bobby to take the first bite. Bobby's face turned red. Then it turned green. He had never tasted fish before. But finally he managed to get a bit into his mouth. He chewed slowly and swallowed. It was delicate and sweet. He licked the buttery sauce from his lips. He took another bite. It was delicious! The Little

*A large basket of seafood mysteriously
appeared on Bobby's doorstep.*

People broke out in cheers and fell to feasting.

Next came steamed clams. These were followed by fried oysters. And finally, there were big, red boiled lobsters. Bobby ate it all and enjoyed every bite. Soon, he was too full to eat another bite.

As people often do after a big meal, Bobby dozed off. Then he fell into a deep sleep. When he awoke, he was under a rosebush. He was back to his own size again. Had it all been a dream? He thought so. But then he found a tiny napkin tucked under his chin. It was stained with butter sauce.

And every week after that, on Friday, a large basket of seafood mysteriously appeared on Bobby's doorstep. He ate well and stayed healthy all his life—on fish.

GREEN DREAMS

Already Patrick was homesick. He leaned against the rail of the ship that was taking him to America. It would be a new world, a new life.

But Ireland is my life, my home, he thought. *Am I leaving too much behind? I'll miss that green and lovely island!*

How could I have turned my back on her! And what of the Little People? I shall miss them more than anything.

Now not everyone believes in the Little People. In fact, there was a time when Patrick himself did not. But one evening, Patrick changed his mind.

The sun had just set. Walking along the seashore that he had known so well, he came to the trees that sheltered his cottage. He turned to look at the moon and stars. As he turned, he bumped his head on a low-hanging branch. Patrick fell. How long did he lie there? He did not know. He did know that when he opened his eyes, he was staring at a mushroom. The mushroom stared back. Then the mushroom said, "Did you hurt yourself?"

Now Patrick wasn't the smartest person alive. But he knew that mushrooms didn't talk. And Patrick was right. It was an elf holding an umbrella.

"What are you looking at, sir?" asked the elf. "Haven't you ever seen an umbrella before?" Patrick closed his eyes and thought. *I hurt my head. Yes, that's it! When you hurt your head, you see things. But you see stars, bright lights, pinwheels—not little men holding umbrellas.*

"All right," said Patrick, "I'm going to open my eyes now. When they are open, I'll see the green grass, the yellow sand, and the blue sea—maybe a mushroom. But that is all! I'm opening one eye. Here comes the other eye." Patrick looked, but he did not see the elf. "Ah now, that's better. My head is clear. I'm all right now."

"Don't get up," said the elf, "I'm standing on your neck."

It was an elf holding an umbrella.

"Oh, don't do that!" exclaimed Patrick.

"You're right," said the elf. "I'm not being very polite. I'll get off now. I beg your pardon."

"It's quite all right," said Patrick. "But may I ask you a question? Are you a little man with an umbrella?"

"What else would I be," asked the elf, "a mushroom?"

"As a matter of fact," said Patrick, "at first, I rather thought you were."

"Mushrooms don't talk," the elf replied.

"You're right about that," agreed Patrick. It was then that he knew he was face to face with one of the Little People.

"And what are you doing with an umbrella? It's not raining," said Patrick.

"It's for the early-morning dew," replied the elf. "Have you noticed I'm a bit small? When a drop of dew plops on me, I get soaking wet."

"Oh, of course," said Patrick. Then he made a grab for the elf.

"What's this all about?" cried the elf as he struggled in Patrick's hand. But Patrick had remembered all the stories. When you see one of the Little People, catch him if you can. Then he has to tell you where his gold is. And he gives you three wishes. But that's only if you say his name backwards. The trick is to learn his name. Patrick used to laugh at these stories. But he wasn't laughing now.

"Tell me where your gold is," demanded Patrick.

"Are you crazy?" asked the elf. "What gold? Gold is where you find it."

"Well then, what's your name?"

"Bubbub," answered the elf.

"Bubbub?" repeated Patrick. "Now that's an odd name. I have to say it backwards, you see, so you stand there

*"What's this all about?" cried the elf as he
struggled in Patrick's hand.*

until I work it out. Then you owe me three wishes."

"You just work on it, Patrick," said the elf. "And while you are testing your brain, I'll set you straight."

"Wait a minute," said Patrick. "Do you have a pencil? Your name is crowded with B's, and I'm getting all mixed up. I need the three wishes, you see. I want to go to America, get there safely, and start a new life."

"In the first place," explained the elf, "you're all confused. The gold is at the end of the rainbow. But the rainbow is richer than all the gold there is. And if you want three wishes, you can have them. But you don't have to be rough about it. As for saying my name backwards, you already have."

"Then I ask you to forgive me," said Patrick.

From that time on, Patrick saw the Little People often. He would sit down with them and tell of his dreams. He watched the sea with them and looked at the stars. Above all, he opened his heart. Soon, all his fears melted away. He learned to love all the things of this world. The Little People showed him the beauty of the earth and sky. They taught him what joy there was in being alive.

But now Patrick was on his way to America, and he was sad. Leaning against the rail of the ship, he saw the Statue of Liberty off in the distance. It was welcoming him. The giant lady was standing near another shore, saying "Hello." But what of the Little People? Would he ever see his friends again?

"*Psst*, Patrick!" whispered a tiny voice. Patrick turned to see who was calling. "Look down here. I haven't grown all

*Patrick saw the Statue of Liberty
off in the distance.*

that much!" It was Bubbub.

Patrick was full of joy. "Ah, my little friend, are you off to America, too? Have you come to give me my three wishes?"

Then Bubbub laughed a kind, gentle laugh. "Why, Patrick, you've had your three wishes! You wished to go to America, get there safely, and start a new life. All three came true. Don't you see, Patrick? Your wishes are your own and *you* make them come true. And everywhere you go can be a home if you want it to be. The grass is green here, too. The sea is blue. The stars and moon smile down as they do in Ireland. You will always have Ireland with you."

So Patrick waved back at the Statue of Liberty. *She's green,* thought Patrick. *She's green and bright with hope.*